The Rainbow Quilt

Iris Howden

Published in association with
The Basic Skills Agency

Hodder & Stoughton

A MEMBER OF THE HODDER HEADLINE GROUP

Acknowledgements
Cover: Barry Downard
Illustrations: Ruth Thomlevold

Orders: please contact Bookpoint Ltd, 130 Milton Park, Abingdon, Oxon OX14 4SB. Telephone: (44) 01235 827720, Fax: (44) 01235 400454. Lines are open from 9.00–6.00, Monday to Saturday, with a 24 hour message answering service. You can also order through our website: www.hodderheadline.co.uk.

British Library Cataloguing in Publication Data
A catalogue record for this title is available from The British Library

ISBN 0 340 87665 4

First published 2003
Impression number 10 9 8 7 6 5 4 3 2 1
Year   2007 2006 2005 2004 2003

Typeset by SX Composing DTP, Rayleigh, Essex.
Printed in Great Britain for Hodder & Stoughton Educational, a division of Hodder Headline, 338 Euston Road, London NW1 3BH by Athenaeum Press, Gateshead, Tyne and Wear.

Contents

1

The Rainbow Quilt

'How was it?' Amy's mother asked.
'Did you enjoy your first day at college?'

'It was OK,' Amy said.
'Is tea ready yet?'
She didn't feel like talking.
It had been a long day.

The college was very big.
There was so much to take in.
– Forms to fill in.
– New classes and new teachers.
– Lots of students.
It wasn't like school.
She knew everyone there.

One girl had been nice – that Asian girl.
Aneeta was her name.
She was just as shy as Amy.
They had gone round together.
– Found their classes together.
– Had lunch together.
Amy really liked her.
She hoped they would be friends.

The weeks passed.
Amy got used to being at college.
She was studying Fashion and Design.
They did a lot of basic things at first.
They learned how to thread a needle.
– How to sew on a button.
– How to use a sewing machine safely.
'I don't want any accidents,'
the tutor said.

Their tutor was quite young.
She wore trendy clothes.
The students called her Jan.

'You two work well together' Jan said
to Amy and Aneeta.
'I'd like you to take part in a project.
Some of the ladies' groups in the town
are making a quilt.
It will be made up of squares.
Each square will be a picture.
A picture that shows
some aspect of the town.
Later it will hang in the town hall.'

'I'm not keen on doing a quilt,'
Amy told Aneeta at lunch time.
'I can't wait to start making clothes.
I want to draw my own designs –
not make some boring old quilt'

'Me too,' Aneeta said.
She wore Punjabi dress.
She showed Amy the latest styles
in a magazine.

'We can't really say no,' said Aneeta.
'Jan chose us to do it.
It will be good practice.
We can try out all kinds of stitches,
and use wool or beads.'

'I suppose so,' Amy said.
'Come over to my house on Saturday.
We'll try and think up some ideas.'

'I'll have to ask my parents,' Aneeta said.
'I'll let you know tomorrow.'

The next day
Aneeta told Amy she could come.
'My dad knows your dad,' she said.
'They met through business.
He knows you are from a good family.'

'He sounds very strict,' Amy said.

'Not really,' Aneeta told her.
'Muslim families protect the girls.'

Amy wanted to know
about the Muslim way of life.
'We learn to read the *Koran*.
That's our holy book,' said Aneeta.
'On a Friday we go to the Mosque.
The imam is our priest – like your vicar.'

'Ramadan is our holy time.
It's a month when we fast.
We don't eat between sunrise and sunset.
When it's over
we have the festival of Eid.
We have a party,
and the children get gifts of money.'

2
Making Plans

On Saturday Aneeta's dad drove her over.
Amy's father went to the door.
The two men shook hands.
'How do you know Aneeta's dad?'
Amy asked.

'He's one of my clients,' he said.
Amy's dad was a rep for an I.T. firm.
Aneeta's father ran his own business.
He had a take-away shop in town.

'My mum will drive you home,' Amy said.
'We're having pizza and salad for tea.'

'Great,' Aneeta said. 'I love pizza.'

Amy and her mum had talked about
what to give Aneeta for tea.
'Is she vegetarian?' Amy's mum asked.

'Not really,' Amy said. 'She eats meat,
but only if it's Halal.
Halal meat is killed in a special way.
Muslims don't eat pork at all.'

The two girls talked
about ideas for the quilt.
'My grandad came here
in the Sixties,' Aneeta said.
'He worked in the cotton mill.
It's closed down now.
I could do a picture of that.'

'I remember the cotton mills.
My aunty worked in one,' Amy's mum said.
'The machines were really noisy.
The girls had to learn to lip read.
You couldn't hear a word anyone said.'

'What about my square?' Amy said.
'My grandfather worked in an office.
That wouldn't make a very good picture.'

'He was in the town band,' Amy's mum said.

'Brilliant!' Amy said. 'I'll do his trumpet.'

The two girls spent some time
making sketches for their squares.
Aneeta drew the cotton mill.
She put in lots of windows,
and some workers in the mill yard.
She drew a canal in front of the mill.

'That looks great,' Amy said.
'What do you think of mine?'
She showed Aneeta her drawing.
It had a cap and a trumpet in the middle.
A sheet of music lay at the back.

'That's really good,' Aneeta said.
'We'll show them to Jan on Monday.
But we have to do two squares each.
What shall we put on the others?'

'We'll think about those later,' Amy said.
'Let's go up to my room.
I'll play you my new CD.'

3
The Gang

The girls walked back from college.
They went through the town centre.
Amy had to catch her bus there.
One day they saw a gang of youths.
They were handing out leaflets.
They had skin-head hair cuts.
They wore big boots.
They had rings in their ears,
and studs through their noses.

Aneeta took Amy's arm.
'Come on,' she said. 'Let's go.
I don't like the look of them.'

12

One of the youths stood in their way.
He would not let them pass.
He handed Amy a leaflet.
'You should read this,' he said.
'Paki lover.'
He spat on the ground.

The girls ran into the bus station.
Aneeta was shaking. She was really upset.

'What was all that about?' Amy asked.

'Read the leaflet,' Aneeta said.

Amy looked at the words at the top.
'KEEP BRITAIN WHITE' it said.
'This is sick,' she said.
She threw it in a bin.
'I didn't think this kind of thing
went on here,' she said.

'Oh yes, it does,' Aneeta told her.

'I've seen them before,' said Aneeta.
'They hang around near where I live.
They like to cause trouble.
They try to pick a fight with our lads.
My dad's worried that my brother
will join an Asian gang.
Some of them want to fight back.'

'How old is Samir?' Amy asked.

'He's fourteen,' Aneeta said.
'He drives my parents mad.
Mind you, he is a bit of a pain.
He wants everything he sees –
new trainers costing £100,
the latest CDs and designer clothes.'

Amy laughed.
'I can't wait to meet him,' she said.

'You'll see him on Saturday,' Aneeta said.
'When you come to tea.'

'I'm looking forward to it,' Amy said.
'I'll see you then. Don't worry.
Those lads are just yobs. They're all talk.'

But on Saturday she was not so sure.
She walked down Aneeta's street.
The same lads were hanging about.
Amy crossed the road.
She ran to the take-away.
Aneeta's dad was in the shop.
'Hello, Amy,' he said.
'Go through to the house.'

Amy went into the living room.
It was full of people.
Aneeta introduced her to them.
'This is my mum,' she said.
'My grandma and my aunt.
These are my cousins Abdal and Samia.
And this pest is my brother Samir.'

Amy said hello to everyone.
She sat on the sofa next to Aneeta.
The older ladies were wearing saris.
Aneeta had a new outfit on.
She was wearing gold ear-rings.
'You look really nice,' Amy said.

Aneeta's mum spread a cloth on the floor.
The ladies brought in lots of dishes.
They laid them out on the cloth.
There was rice and meat, fish curry,
kebabs and dishes of vegetables.
'My mum loves cooking,' Aneeta said.

Aneeta's mum handed Amy a plate.
'Help yourself,' she said.
'Try a bit of everything.
There's halva and sweet rice to follow.'

'Thank you very much,'
Amy said when she left.
'I've had a lovely time.'

4
The Riot

On Monday Amy was eating her breakfast.
Her mum was in the lounge.
She was watching the news on TV.
She shouted to Amy.
'Come quick, Amy. Look at this.'
Amy ran through to the lounge.
The news was all about a riot.
It was in their town.

Amy saw Aneeta's street on the screen.
It looked a mess.
Cars had been set alight.
Shop windows had been broken.

The pub on the corner
had been burned out.
The walls were black with smoke.
There had been a fight the night before.
Gangs of white and Asian youths had met.
They had thrown bricks at each other.

Amy watched in horror.
'I must get to college,' she told her mum.
'I want to make sure that Aneeta's okay.'

'I'll give you a lift,' her mum said.

Aneeta was not there for the first class.
Amy rang her mobile.
There was no reply.
She sent her a text message.
By lunch-time there was no answer.

Amy went round to Aneeta's house.
She ran most of the way.
There were police cars in the street.

She went into the take-away.
Aneeta's grandma was there alone.
She was sweeping up broken glass.
The shop window had been broken.

'What happened?' Amy asked.
'Where is everyone?'

The old lady's eyes were full of tears.
'Aneeta's in hospital,' she told Amy.
'She was hit on the head with a brick.
Her mother is there with her.
And Samir was in the fight.
The police arrested him.
His dad's at the police station now.'

Amy took a bus to the hospital.
She found Aneeta's ward.
Her friend looked very pale.
She had a bandage round her head.
'How are you?' Amy asked.

'She has a nasty cut on her head,'
Aneeta's mother told Amy.
'Aneeta went out to find Samir.
To try and stop him fighting.
She'll be in hospital for a few days,'
said Aneeta's mother.

'I'll come back tomorrow,' Amy said.
'Is there anything you need?'

'Can you bring my quilt square?' Aneeta said.
'I could sew that while I'm here.'

Amy laughed. 'You're keen,' she said.

She went back the next day.
She took Aneeta's sewing.
She brought flowers and magazines.
The other students had sent them.
They had all signed a Get Well card.
'Hurry up and get better,' Amy said.
'I really miss you.'

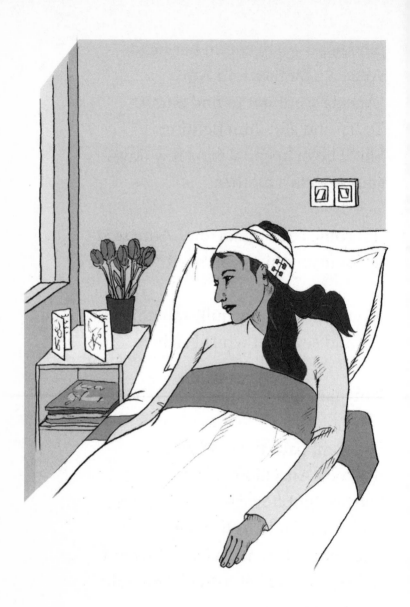

5
A Special Day

Months later there was a special day.
A multi-faith service was held in church.
People from every group in town came.
The imam was there from the mosque.
There were Jews and Hindus and Catholics.
There were white people, black people,
Chinese and Asians.

Amy and Aneeta sat in the front row.
Their parents were behind them.
Samir and Aneeta's Grandma was there.
There were students from the college.
Jan and some of the other tutors came too.

At the front hung the quilt.
It looked wonderful.
There were squares with so many pictures.
– A football strip for the town team.
– Flowers and trees for the park.
– Buses and trains to show transport.
– Cups and plates for a local china factory.
– Fruit and veg on a market stall.
– Books in a library.
– Swings in a play-ground.
It was all the colours of the rainbow.

The vicar spoke to the people.
'We are here today to give thanks.
Our town has seen some bad times.
There was a riot in the streets.
Hate in people's hearts,' he said.
'Now things have changed for the better.
People have come together,
to stamp out racism,
and to work for the good of the community.'

He pointed to the quilt.
'This beautiful work of art sums it up.
It shows the daily life of our town.
It shows some of our history.
It will remind us not to let
evil things happen here again.'

He put his hand on the last two squares.
Those done by Amy and Aneeta.
After the riot.
They had worked on them together.
One showed red flames and cars on fire.
It showed the burnt out pub,
its walls black with smoke.

The second one had a church
standing next to a mosque.
A rainbow in the sky linked the two.
The vicar pointed to it.
'This rainbow is sign of hope,' he said.
'Hope for a better future.'

After the service they all went
into the church hall.
There were tea and cakes laid on.
'Well done,' Jan told the girls.
'That quilt is a lovely piece of work.'
She spoke to their parents.
She told them how well they were doing.

Amy and Aneeta sat down to eat.
'Samir's very quiet,' Amy said.

'He's on his best behaviour,' Aneeta said.
'He has been ever since the riot.
He got a fright
when the police arrested him.
They gave him a good telling off.
The imam spoke to all the
Asian boys as well.
Samir blames himself for my accident.
He hasn't stepped out of line since.
My mum and dad think it's great.'

Amy laughed.

'So some good came out of it,' she said.
'What's our next project?'

'Not a quilt. That's for sure,' Aneeta said.
'I never want to see another square
as long as I live.'